I Live in Brooklyn

For Jo and Gen

The text of this book is set in 13-point Stone Serif.
The illustrations are watercolor.

Library of Congress Cataloging-in-Publication Data
Takabayashi, Mari, 1960–
I live in Brooklyn / written and illustrated by Mari Takabayashi.
p. cm.
Summary: Six-year-old Michelle, who lives in Brooklyn, New York,
describes what she and her family and friends do throughout the year.
ISBN 0-618-30899-7
[1. Family life—New York (N.Y.)—Fiction. 2. Year—Fiction.
3. New York (N.Y.)—Fiction.] I. Title.
PZ7.T14124Iae 2004   [E]—dc22   2003012292

Printed in China
LEO   10 9
4500516763

Chinese New Year in Manhattan

Lucy and I and our lemonade stand

I Live in Brooklyn

Written & illustrated by

Mari Takabayashi

Houghton Mifflin Company Boston

The big picture book corner at Brooklyn's central library

The Brooklyn Botanic Gardens in spring

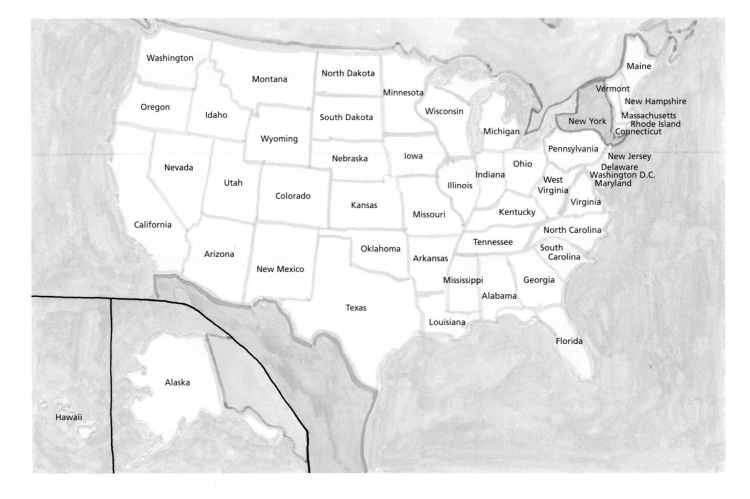

Map of Brooklyn

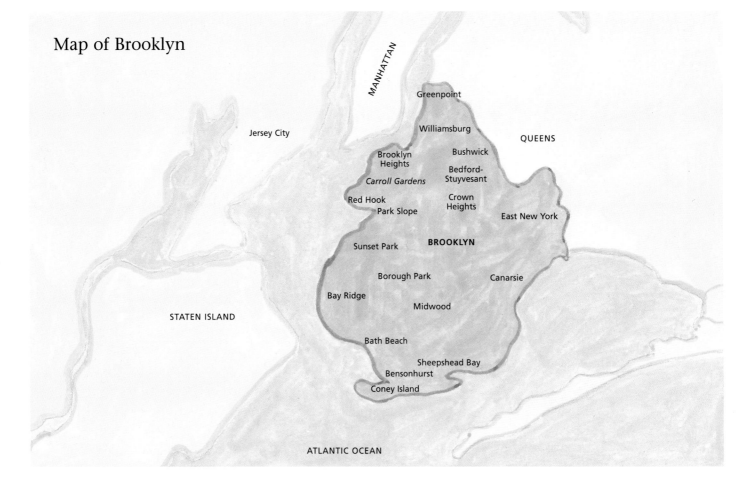

My name is Michelle. I am six years old. I live in Brooklyn, New York. Brooklyn is one of the five boroughs of New York City. A river separates us from Manhattan.

My neighborhood is called Carroll Gardens.

At night, when I'm in my bed, I can hear the ships blowing their whistles.

In my house, Daddy wakes up first every morning, then my mom and little sister, Lucy. I am always last. My mom has to wake me up because I'm usually deep in a fun dream. Mom makes breakfast quickly and starts to get ready for work. My grandma arrives to take care of Lucy while Mom and Dad are at work.

I take the B75 bus with my mom. She drops me off at school and then goes on to her office. The bus comes to our corner at 8:15 sharp. I know we should leave the house a little early, but somehow we have to run to catch the bus almost every day. Mom says, "Good exercise, Michelle!" after we get on.

If I get to school early, I play on the playground. It's fun, even for just a few minutes.

When school starts, I find my best friends, Mary and Rosa. Then we say the Pledge of Allegiance and our teacher, Mrs. Betty, starts the class.

Free choice time is the best part of the day. We get to choose whatever we want to do—computer, drawing, games, puzzles. I pick drawing every time.

I also love the school bake sales. My grandmother helps me make cookies to sell. Everybody brings a quarter and buys one treat for a snack.

We are always so excited to be on the bus. It gets pretty noisy until Ms. Betty says, "Be quiet! Calm down, everybody!"

We take a field trip almost every month. The school bus takes us to so many places—the aquarium, zoo, theater...

One day we went to the Central Park Zoo. My favorite animals are the penguins. Mary and I were impressed that they can swim so fast.

The American Museum of Natural History is the best! I wish I could stay there for a few days and see everything.

Every fall we spend a day apple-picking in upstate New York.
I like very crisp apples.

A few weeks later, we visit the pumpkin patch and choose
a few huge pumpkins for jack-o'-lanterns.

Once in a while we have a snow day in Brooklyn. Daddy starts to shovel the sidewalk in front of our house as soon as the snow stops, so no one will slip.

Then we bundle up and go to Prospect Park. We bring our sled and slide down the hill over and over until we are cold and our feet are wet.

Daddy takes me window shopping on Fifth Avenue every year. It is fun to see Santa Claus standing in the crowd with his bell.

We spend Christmas Day at my grandparents' house. My grandma is a good cook. She cooks a feast of ham, chicken with stuffing, salad, chocolate cake, and cookies.

The Christmas tree stands start to appear on the street corners around the first week of December. We always buy our tree from the same farm from Vermont.

My mom and Lucy and I make origami Christmas ornaments. We make baskets, snowmen, a little house, peppermint sticks, and Christmas stockings.

My mom sewed my Halloween costume. She is so good at creating things. This year I am Little Red Riding Hood. Kate, Sam, Jiji, Lena, and I go trick-or-treating in our neighborhood. We collect a lot of candy! My mom says, "You can eat as much as you want tonight. But starting tomorrow you have to choose only one piece of candy a day."

We also go to the Prospect Park skate rink every weekend in the winter. We go in the morning because it will be very crowded by the afternoon.

Whenever my mom makes a sandwich, she saves the edges of the bread for us so that we can feed the ducks in the park. They are always hungry.

I like having playdates with my friends. The problem is, Lucy often bothers us.

My mom reads to us before we go to sleep each night. Lucy and I may choose one or two picture books each. I like folk tales.

I go to swimming class every Monday. I couldn't swim at all when I started taking lessons. Now I can do the forward crawl.

Sometimes my grandma takes us to a restaurant after swimming. Lucy and I order something sweet and Grandma always has coffee.

My Favorite Stuff

Handmade tea set for my dollhouse. It's very small.

Frame that my grandpa painted

Doll that Grandma made when I was born

Diary

Memos.
Whenever I go out, I bring my memo pad and pencil.

Yarn, left over from my grandma. I know how to make yarn pompoms.

Ocarina, I can't play this yet, but someday I hope to because it sounds so beautiful.

Handmade box

Origami, with colored figures

Erasers

Heart-shaped stone I found at a creek

Buttons

Matryoshka dolls that my friend Misha brought back from Russia

Soap

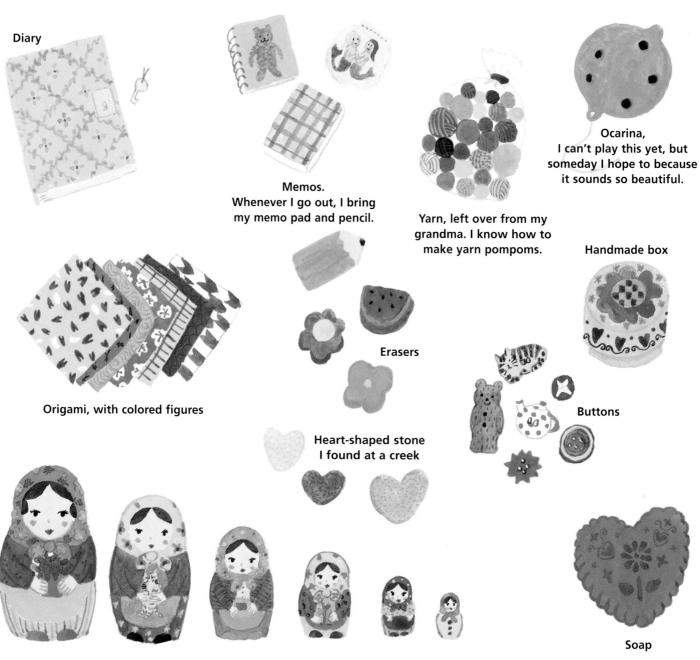

What is the smell of the city? There are so many tasty smells along the city streets.

Shish kebabs

Honey nuts

Hot dogs and pretzels

Coffee, bagels, and donuts

When the weather turns warm in the spring, we bicycle to Prospect Park, where there is a zoo, a playground, a carousel, a lake with boats, and lots of trails and grass.

After we eat the lunch my mom packed, we lie down. I see clouds like cotton candy in the blue sky and hear a mother bird calling her babies.

My grandparents live one block from our house. My grandpa became an artist after he retired. He likes to draw flowers. I often draw with him. I feel like I can draw better when he is sitting next to me and teaching me.

My school summer vacation lasts more than two months. I play with my
neighbors outside after dinner every night. It stays light until eight-thirty.
We play hopscotch, jump rope, and draw on the sidewalk with chalk.

On the Fourth of July, we go up to our roof to watch the fireworks with our neighbors. The fireworks are so beautiful. Somehow I feel a little sad when they are over.

My mom and I go to the farmer's market in Union Square before my aunt comes to visit during the summer. Sometimes the lettuce has holes from

caterpillars because it is organic. Soon our basket is filled with bunches of
flowers, vegetables, bread, homemade jam, and fresh eggs.

Mom and Dad take us to the beach at Coney Island every summer. We wear swimsuits under our clothes. The last stop on the F train is Coney Island. The F line runs above the ground in Brooklyn, and I like to look out the window. Lucy always falls asleep on the train.

We go to the amusement park after playing on the beach. My favorite ride is the Ferris wheel. I love the thrill and the view. We go home sandy, sticky, and tired.

Finally—I turn seven! This year we go bowling for my birthday party.
I invited five friends: Mary, Rosa, Jiji, Beth, and Alex.

Afterward we all come back to my house for ice cream cake. I feel like
such a happy and lucky girl! Thank you, Mom and Dad!